Sometimes I Dream Horses

Jeanne Whitehouse Peterson

Pictures by Eleanor Schick

Harper & Row, Publishers

This book belongs to

Kayleigh Kruger

Sometimes I Dream Horses
Text copyright © 1987 by Jeanne Whitehouse Peterson
Illustrations copyright © 1987 by Eleanor Schick
Printed in the U.S.A. All rights reserved.
1 2 3 4 5 6 7 8 9 10
First Edition

Library of Congress Cataloging-in-Publication Data
Peterson, Jeanne Whitehouse.
  Sometimes I dream horses.

  Summary: A little girl's dream of riding a horse
comes true on her grandmother's ranch in the southwest.
  [1. Horses—Fiction. 2. Dreams—Fiction.
3. Grandmothers—Fiction.] I. Schick, Eleanor,
1942-   ill. II. Title.
PZ7.P4444So 1987   [E]   83-47710
ISBN 0-06-024712-6
ISBN 0-06-024713-4 (lib. bdg.)

In memory of my grandmother Bessie
J.W.P.

To a special family and the magic of their land
E.S.

To Kayleigh, a lover of Horses!
Love, Aunt Jean XO   2011

After my story,
and after my bath,
and after "good night"
to the cow and her calf,
and SOMETIMES after a ride
on the hired man's knee,
then Grandma and I
climb the old, creaky stairs.
We fold my clothes
on the wicker chair,
and I slide DEEP DOWN
between the cold sheets.

"I'll be by the fire," I hear
Grandma whisper.

Then I lie with my nose
pressed close to the window.
I rub the satin curtain
against my cheek.
There are a million stars
to count,
and one old Uncle Moon
rising over the hill.

I shut my eyes,
waiting to sleep,
because—

SOMETIMES
I dream
horses!

Yes, sometimes when the wind

tugs at my covers

and tickles my chin,

I dream dark horses

leap over my bed

on their way

to the edge of the mesa.

Or sometimes, our new colt

follows me

into the hidden willows.

Together we splash

in the stream.

And SOMETIMES,
in my favorite dream,
Grandma's own White Jamal
whinnies beneath my window.

He waits patiently
to take me—
past moon, past stars.
We race the brilliant sunrise.

Mornings, I slide from my bed
to the smells of frying bacon,
baking bread.

I take big bites, then help
to dry the dishes.
Grandma makes a pot of tea
and listens to my dreams.

We watch George bring the plow horses
back from the field.
"Sure could use help!" he calls,
so I run to the barn
to help with the harness.
I rub the mud from the backs
of their legs.

I touch his hand as we turn them out.
"Do you dream horses?" I ask.

George swings me high
over his head—
so high I see the fishing flies
hooked in his hat.
" 'Tis FLYING dreams I have!"
he says as he sets me down.
"Sometimes I'm a pigeon
circling the barn!"

I find Grandma hanging sheets
on the clothesline.
As I hold the basket, I ask,
"Do birds dream?"
"Do pigs?" she answers back.
It sounds so funny,
we both laugh.

But later I see George's old dog,
Pete, wiggle and whimper
in his sleep.

Maybe he dreams rabbits, I think.

After supper Grandma takes me
for a walk in the field.
"Here are two sugar cubes,"
she says, "one for you
and one for White Jamal."
I watch him trot to us
when she calls.

Gently I rub the softness
of his nose
and feel him breathe
on my fingers.

"Please dream of me,"
I whisper.

Grandma touches my shoulder.
"Hold fast to his mane," she says
as she boosts me up,
and suddenly: HERE I AM!
Higher than the fence posts!
Higher than Grandma's head!

With each step I feel his muscles
stretch and glide.
I slip from side
to side,
but hold on as tight as I can
with my knees
and damp fingers.

And I do not mind the way
his tail whisks against my legs,
or how the breeze
smells of horses
because—

I AM RIDING WHITE JAMAL!
Slowly we follow Grandma
to the barn.

"There," she says
as she lifts me down.
"Tomorrow you may brush him
and feed him,
and I will teach you to ride
to the canyon and back."

I am so happy, my wiggly legs
can hardly stand.
"Just like our new colt!"
She laughs.

Later, as we sit beside the fire,
Grandma takes a golden frame
from her desk.
On one side is a mirror,
on the other, a picture of a girl
riding a great white horse.

Grandma sits down and pulls
me onto her lap.
"Guess who?" she asks,
holding the photo
close to the lamp.

"GOLDILOCKS?" I tease.
"THE QUEEN OF ENGLAND?"

"No!" Grandma says. "It's me!
On the day *I* first learned to ride
to the canyon!"
And I believe her, because the girl
is just my size,
only she is wearing a long skirt
and a wide-brimmed hat.

Grandma shows me her scrapbook,
filled with tiny sketches.
She teaches me a pony song
she used to like to sing.

Then Grandma and I climb
the old, creaky stairs.
We fold my clothes
on the wicker chair,
and I slide deep down
between the cold sheets.

There are a million stars
to count,
and one old Uncle Moon
rising over the hill.

Below us, a new colt
is sleeping by his mother.
And in the barn, White Jamal
watches for tomorrow.

Just before she leaves,
Grandma places her picture
by my pillow.
She kisses my cheek
and gives my fingers
a squeeze.

I shut my eyes
waiting to sleep,
because—

SOMETIMES I DREAM HORSES!